Philippa
Pearce

At the River-Gates
and Other
Supernatural Stories

D1136838

PENGUIN BOOKS

PENGUIN BOOKS

Published by the Penguin Group
Penguin Books Ltd, 27 Wrights Lane, London W8 5TZ, England
Penguin Books USA Inc., 375 Hudson Street, New York, New York 10014, USA
Penguin Books Australia Ltd, Ringwood, Victoria, Australia
Penguin Books Canada Ltd, 10 Alcorn Avenue, Toronto, Ontario, Canada M4V 3B2
Penguin Books (NZ) Ltd, 182–190 Wairau Road, Auckland 10, New Zealand

Penguin Books Ltd, Registered Offices: Harmondsworth, Middlesex, England

**First published in *The Shadow-Cage and Other Tales of the Supernatural* by
Kestrel Books 1977**
Published in Puffin Books 1978

This collection published in Penguin Books 1996
1 3 5 7 9 10 8 6 4 2

Filmset in Lasercomp Bembo by
Datix International Limited, Bungay, Suffolk
Made and printed in England by Clays Ltd, St Ives plc

Contents

At the River-Gates

LOTS of sisters I had (said the old man), good girls, too; and one elder brother. Just the one. We were at either end of the family: the eldest, my brother John – we always called him Beany, for some reason; then the girls, four of them; then me. I was Tiddler, and the reason for that was plain.

Our father was a flour miller, and we lived just beside the mill. It was a water-mill, built right over the river, with the mill-wheel underneath. To understand what happened that wild night, all those years ago, you have to understand a bit about the working of the mill-stream. About a hundred yards before the river reached the mill, it divided: the upper river flowed on to power the mill, as I've said; the lower river, leaving the upper river through sluice-gates, flowed to one side of the mill and past it; and then the upper and lower rivers joined up again well below the mill. The sluice-gates could be opened or shut by the miller to let more or less water through from the upper to the lower river. You can see the use of that: the miller controlled the flow of water to power his mill; he could also draw off any floodwaters that came down.

Being a miller's son, I can never remember not understanding that. I was a little tiddler, still at school, when my brother, Beany, began helping my father in the mill. He was as good as a man, my father said. He was strong, and he learnt the feel of the grain, and he was clever with the mill machinery, and he got on with the other men in the mill – there were only ten of them, counting two carters. He understood the gates, of course, and how to get just the right head of water for the mill. And he liked it all: he liked the work he did, and the life; he liked the mill, and the river, and the long river-bank. One day he'd be the miller after my father, everyone said.

I was too young to feel jealousy about that; but I would never have felt jealous of Beany, because Beany was the best brother you could have had. I loved and admired him more than anyone I knew or could imagine knowing. He was very good to me.

He used to take me with him when you might have thought a little boy would have been in the way. He took me with him when he went fishing, and he taught me to fish. I learnt patience, then, from Beany. There were plenty of roach and dace in the river; and sometimes we caught trout or pike; and once we caught an eel, and I was first of all terrified and then screaming with excitement at the way it whipped about on the bank, but Beany held it and killed it, and my mother made it into eel-pie. He knew about the fish in the river, and the little creatures, too. He showed me fresh-water shrimps, and leeches – 'Look, Tiddler, they make themselves into croquet-hoops when they want to go anywhere!' and he showed me the little underwater cottages of caddis-worms. He knew where to get good watercress for Sunday tea – you could eat watercress from our river, in those days.

We had an old boat on the river, and Beany would take it upstream to inspect the banks for my father. The banks had to be kept sound: if there was a breach, it would let the water escape and reduce the water-power for the mill. Beany took Jess, our dog, with him in the boat, and he often took me. Beany was the only person I've ever known who could point out a kingfisher's nest in the river-bank. He knew about birds. He once showed me a flycatcher's nest in the brickwork below the sluice-gates, just above where the water dashed and roared at its highest. Once, when we were in the boat, he pointed ahead to an otter in the water. I held on to Jess's collar then.

It was Beany who taught me to swim. One summer it was hotter than anyone remembered, and Beany was going from the mill up to the gates to shut in more water. Jess was following him, and as he went he gave me a wink, so I followed too, although I didn't know why. As usual, he opened the gates with the great iron spanner, almost as long in the handle as he was tall. Then he went down to the pool in the lower river, as if to see the water-level there. But as he went he was unbuttoning his flour-whitened waist-coat; by the time he reached the pool he was naked, and he dived straight in. He came up with his hair plastered over his eyes, and he called to me: 'Come on, Tiddler! Just time for a swimming lesson!' Jess sat on the bank and watched us.

Jess was really my father's dog, but she attached herself to Beany. She loved Beany. Everyone loved Beany, and he was good to everyone. Especially, as I've said, to me. Just sometimes he'd say, 'I'm off on my own now, Tiddler,' and then I knew better than to ask to go with him. He'd go sauntering up the river-bank by himself, except for Jess at his heels. I don't think he did anything very particular when he went off on his own. Just the river and the river-bank were happiness enough for him.

He was still not old enough to have got himself a girl, which might have changed things a bit; but he wasn't too young to go to the War. The War broke out in 1914, when I was still a boy, and Beany went.

It was sad without Beany; but it was worse than that. I was too young to understand then; but, looking back, I realize what was wrong. There was fear in the house. My parents became gloomy and somehow secret. So many young men were being killed at the

5

Front. Other families in the village had had word of a son's death. The news came in a telegram. I overheard my parents talking of those deaths, those telegrams, although not in front of the girls or me. I saw my mother once, in the middle of the morning, kneeling by Beany's bed, praying.

So every time Beany came home on leave, alive, we were lucky.

But when Beany came, he was different. He loved us as much, but he was different. He didn't play with me as he used to do; he would sometimes stare at me as though he didn't see me. When I shouted 'Beany!' and rushed at him, he would start as if he'd woken up. Then he'd smile, and be good to me, almost as he used to be. But, more often than he used to, he'd be off all by himself up the river-bank, with Jess at his heels. My mother, who longed to have him within her sight for every minute of his leave, used to watch him go, and sigh. Once I heard her say to my father that the river-bank did Beany good, as if he were sickening for some strange disease. Once one of the girls was asking Beany about the Front and the trenches, and he was telling her this and that, and we were all interested, and suddenly he stopped and said, 'No. It's hell.' And walked away alone, up the green, quiet river-bank. I suppose if one place was hell, then the other was heaven to him.

After Beany's leaves were over, the mill-house was gloomy again; and my father had to work harder, without Beany's help in the mill. Nowadays he had to work the gates all by himself, a thing that Beany had been taking over from him. If the gates needed working at night, my father and Beany had always gone there together. My mother hated it nowadays when my father had to go to the gates alone at night: she was afraid he'd slip and fall in the water, and, although he could swim, accidents could happen to a man alone in the dark. But, of course, my father wouldn't let her come with him, or any of my sisters, and I was still considered much too young. That irked me.

Well, one season had been very dry and the river level had dropped. The gates were kept shut to get up a head of water for the mill. Then clouds began to build up heavily on the horizon, and my father said he was sure it was going to rain; but it didn't. All day storms rumbled in the distance. In the evening the rain began. It rained steadily: my father had already been once to the gates to open the flashes. He was back at home, drying off in front of the fire. The rain still drove against the windows. My mother said, 'It can't come down worse than this.' She and my sisters were still up with my father. Even I wasn't in bed, although I was supposed to have been. No one could have slept for the noise of the rain.

Suddenly the storm grew worse – much worse. It seemed to explode over our heads. We heard a pane of glass in the skylight over the stairs shatter with the force of it, and my sisters ran with buckets to catch the water pouring through. Oddly, my mother didn't go to see the damage: she stayed with my father, watching him like a lynx. He was fidgeting up and down, paying no attention to the skylight either, and suddenly he said he'd have to go up to the gates again and open everything to carry all possible floodwater into the lower river. This was what my mother had been dreading. She made a great outcry, but she knew it was no use. My father put on his tarpaulin jacket again and took his oil lamp and a thick stick — I don't know why, nor did he, I think. Jess always hated being out in the rain, but she followed him. My mother watched him from the back door, lamenting, and urging him to be careful. A few steps from the doorway and you couldn't see him any longer for the driving rain.

My mother's lingering at the back door gave me my chance. I got my boots on and an oilskin cape I had (I wasn't a fool, even if I was little) and I whipped out of the front door and worked my way round in the shelter of the house to the back and then took the path my father had taken to the river, and made a dash for it, and caught up with my father and Jess, just as they were turning up the way towards the gates. I held on to Jess's tail for quite a bit before my father noticed me. He was terribly angry, of course, but he didn't want to turn back with me, and he didn't like to send me back alone, and perhaps in his heart of hearts he was glad of a little human 9 company on such a night. So we all three struggled up to the gates together. Just by the gates my father found me some shelter between a tree-trunk and a stack of drift-wood. There I crouched, with Jess to keep me company.

I was too small to help my father with the gates, but there was one thing I could do. He told me to hold his lamp so that the light shone on the gates and what he was doing. The illumination was very poor, partly because of the driving rain, but at least it was better than nothing, and anyway my father knew those gates by heart. Perhaps he gave me the job of holding the light so that I had something to occupy my mind and keep me from being afraid.

There was plenty to be afraid of on that night of storm.

Directing what light I could on to my father also directed and concentrated my attention on him. I could see his laborious motions as he heaved the great spanner into place. Then he began to try to rack up with it, but the wind and the rain were so strong that 10 I could see he was having the greatest difficulty. Once

I saw him stagger sideways nearly into the blackness of the river. Then I wanted to run out from my shelter and try to help him, but he had strictly forbidden me to do any such thing, and I knew he was right.

Young as I was, I knew – it came to me as I watched him – that he couldn't manage the gates alone in that storm. I suppose he was a man already just past the prime of his strength: the wind and the rain were beating him; the river would beat him.

I shone the light as steadily as I could, and gripped Jess by the collar, and I think I prayed.

I was so frightened then that, afterwards, when I wasn't frightened, I could never be sure of what I had seen, or what I thought I had seen, or what I imagined I had seen. Through the confusion of the storm I saw my father struggling and staggering, and, as I peered and peered, my vision seemed to blur and to double, so that I began sometimes to see one man, sometimes two. My father seemed to have a shadow-self besides himself, who steadied him, heaved with him, worked with him, and at last together they had opened the sluice-gates and let the flood through.

When it was done, my father came back to where Jess and I were, and leant against the tree. He was gasping for breath and exhausted, and had a look on his face that I cannot describe. From his expression I knew that he had *felt* the shadow with him, just as I had seen it. And Jess was agitated too, straining against my hold, whining.

I looked past my father, and I could still see something by the sluice-gates: a shadow that had separated itself from my father, and lingered there. I don't know how I could have seen it in the darkness. I don't know. My father slowly turned and looked in the direction that he saw me looking. The shadow began to move away from the gates, away from us; it began to go up the long river-bank beyond the gates, into the darkness there. It seemed to me that the rain and the wind stilled a little as it went.

Jess wriggled from my grasp and was across the gates and up the river-bank, following the vanished shadow. I had made no move, uttered no word, but my father said to me, 'Let them go!' I looked up at him, and his face was streaming with tears as well as with rain.

12

He took my hand and we fought our way back to the house. The whole house was lit up, to light us home, and my mother stood at the back door, waiting. She gave a cry of horror when she saw me with my father; and then she saw his face, and her own went quite white. He stumbled into her arms, and he sobbed and sobbed. I didn't know until that night that grown men could cry. My mother led my father indoors, and I don't know what talk they had together. My sisters looked after me, dried me, scolded me, put me to bed.

The next day the telegram came to say that Beany had been killed in action in Flanders.

It was some time after that that Jess came home. She was wet through, and my mother thought she was ill, for she sat shivering by the fire, and for two days would neither eat nor drink. My father said: 'Let her be.'

I'm an old man: it all happened so many years ago, but I've never forgotten my brother Beany. He was so good to us all.

The Shadow-Cage

THE little green stoppered bottle had been waiting in the earth a long time for someone to find it. Ned Challis found it. High on his tractor as he ploughed the field, he'd been keeping a look-out, as usual, for whatever might turn up. Several times there had been worked flints; once, one of an enormous size.

Now sunlight glimmering on glass caught his eye. He stopped the tractor, climbed down, picked the bottle from the earth. He could tell at once that it wasn't all that old. Not as old as the flints that he'd taken to the museum in Castleford. Not as old as a coin he had once found, with the head of a Roman emperor on it. Not very old; but old.

Perhaps just useless old . . .

He held the bottle in the palm of his hand and thought of throwing it away. The lip of it was chipped badly, and the stopper of cork or wood had sunk into the neck. With his fingernail he tried to move it. The stopper had hardened into stone, and stuck there. Probably no one would ever get it out now without breaking the bottle. But then, why should anyone want to unstopper the bottle? It was empty, or as good as empty. The bottom of the inside of the bottle was dirtied with something blackish and scaly that also clung a little to the sides.

He wanted to throw the bottle away, but he didn't. He held it in one hand while the fingers of the other cleaned the remaining earth from the outside. When he had cleaned it, he didn't fancy the bottle any more than before; but he dropped it into his pocket. Then he climbed the tractor and started off again.

At that time the sun was high in the sky, and the tractor was working on Whistlers' Hill, which is part of Belper's Farm, fifty yards below Burnt House. As the tractor moved on again, the gulls followed again, rising and falling in their flights, wheeling over the disturbed earth, looking for live things, for food; for good things.

That evening, at tea, Ned Challis brought the bottle out and set it on the table by the loaf of bread. His wife looked at it suspiciously: 'Another of your dirty old things for that museum?'

Ned said: 'It's not museum-stuff. Lisa can have it to take to school. I don't want it.'

Mrs Challis pursed her lips, moved the loaf further away from the bottle, and went to refill the tea-pot.

Lisa took the bottle in her hand. 'Where'd you get it, Dad?'

'Whistlers' Hill. Just below Burnt House.' He frowned suddenly as he spoke, as if he had remembered something.

'What's it got inside?'

'Nothing. And if you try getting the stopper out, that'll break.'

So Lisa didn't try. Next morning she took it to school; but she didn't show it to anyone. Only her cousin Kevin saw it, and that was before school and by accident. He always called for Lisa on his way to school – there was no other company on that country road – and he saw her pick up the bottle from the table, where her mother had left it the night before, and put it into her anorak pocket.

'What was that?' asked Kevin.

'You saw. A little old bottle.'

'Let's see it again – properly.' Kevin was younger than Lisa, and she sometimes indulged him; so she took the bottle out and let him hold it.

At once he tried the stopper.

'Don't,' said Lisa. 'You'll only break it.'

'What's inside?'

'Nothing. Dad found it on Whistlers'.'

'It's not very nice, is it?'

'What do you mean, "Not very nice"?'

'I don't know. But let me keep it for a bit. Please, Lisa.'

On principle Lisa now decided not to give in. 'Certainly not. Give it back.'

He did, reluctantly. 'Let me have it just for today, at school. Please.'

'No.'

'I'll give you something if you'll let me have it. I'll not let anyone else touch it; I'll not let them see it. I'll keep it safe. Just for today.'

'You'd only break it. No. What could you give me, anyway?'

'My week's pocket-money.'

'No. I've said no and I mean no, young Kev.'

'I'd give you that little china dog you like.'

'The one with the china kennel?'

'Yes.'

'The china dog with the china kennel – you'd give me both?'

'Yes.'

'Only for half the day, then,' said Lisa. 'I'll let you have it after school-dinner – look out for me in the playground. Give it back at the end of school. Without fail. And you be careful with it.'

So the bottle travelled to school in Lisa's anorak pocket, where it bided its time all morning. After school-dinner Lisa met Kevin in the playground and they withdrew together to a corner which was well away from the crowded climbing-frame and the infants' sandpit and the rest. Lisa handed the bottle over. 'At the end of school, mind, without fail. And if we miss each other then,' – for Lisa, being in a higher class, came out of school slightly later than Kevin – 'then you must drop it in at ours as you pass. Promise.'

'Promise.'

They parted. Kevin put the bottle into his pocket. He didn't know why he'd wanted the bottle, but he had. Lots of things were like that. You needed them for a bit; and then you didn't need them any longer.

He had needed this little bottle very much.

He left Lisa and went over to the climbing-frame, where his friends already were. He had set his foot on a rung when he thought suddenly how easy it would be for the glass bottle in his trouser pocket to be smashed against the metal framework. He stepped down again and went over to the fence that separated the playground from the farmland beyond. Tall tussocks of grass grew along it, coming through from the open fields and fringing the very edge of the asphalt. He looked round: Lisa had already gone in, and no one else was watching. He put his hand into his pocket and took it out again with the bottle concealed in the fist. He stooped as if to examine an insect on a tussock, and slipped his hand into the middle of it and left the bottle there, well hidden.

He straightened up and glanced around. Since no 19

one was looking in his direction, his action had been unobserved; the bottle would be safe. He ran back to the climbing-frame and began to climb, jostling and shouting and laughing, as he and his friends always did. He forgot the bottle.

He forgot the bottle completely.

It was very odd, considering what a fuss he had made about the bottle, that he should have forgotten it; but he did. When the bell rang for the end of playtime, he ran straight in. He did not think of the bottle then, or later. At the end of afternoon school, he did not remember it; and he happened not to see Lisa, who would surely have reminded him.

Only when he was nearly home, and passing the Challises' house, he remembered. He had faithfully promised – and had really meant to keep his promise. But he'd broken it, and left the bottle behind. If he turned and went back to school now, he would meet Lisa, and she would have to be told . . . By the time he got back to the school playground, all his friends would have gone home: the caretaker would be there, and perhaps a late teacher or two, and they'd all want to know what he was up to. And when he'd got the bottle and dropped it in at the Challises', Lisa would scold him all over again. And when he got home at last, he would be very late for his tea, and his mother would be angry.

As he stood by the Challises' gate, thinking, it seemed best, since he had messed things up anyway, to go straight home and leave the bottle to the next day. So he went home.

He worried about the bottle for the rest of the day, without having the time or the quiet to think about it very clearly. He knew that Lisa would assume he had just forgotten to leave it at her house on the way home. He half expected her to turn up after tea, to claim it; but she didn't. She would have been angry enough about his having forgotten to leave it; but what about her anger tomorrow on the way to school, when she found that he had forgotten it altogether – abandoned it in the open playground? He thought of hurrying straight past her house in the morning; but he would never manage it. She would be on the look-out.

He saw that he had made the wrong decision earlier. He ought, at all costs, to have gone back to the playground to get the bottle.

He went to bed, still worrying. He fell asleep, and his worry went on, making his dreaming unpleasant in a nagging way. He must be quick, his dreams seemed to nag. *Be quick . . .*

Suddenly he was wide awake. It was very late. The sound of the television being switched off must have woken him. Quietness. He listened to the rest of the family going to bed. They went to bed and to sleep. Silence. They were all asleep now, except for him. He couldn't sleep.

Then, as abruptly as if someone had lifted the top of his head like a lid and popped the idea in, he saw that this time – almost the middle of the night – was the perfect time for him to fetch the bottle. He knew by heart the roads between home and school; he would not be afraid. He would have plenty of time. When he reached the school, the gate to the playground would be shut, but it was not high: in the past, by daylight, he and his friends had often climbed it. He would go into the playground, find the correct tussock of grass, get the bottle, bring it back, and have it ready to give to Lisa on the way to school in the morning. She would be angry, but only moderately angry. She would never know the whole truth.

He got up and dressed quickly and quietly. He began to look for a pocket-torch, but gave up when he realized that would mean opening and shutting drawers and cupboards. Anyway, there was a moon tonight, and he knew his way, and he knew the school playground. He couldn't go wrong.

He let himself out of the house, leaving the door on the latch for his return. He looked at his watch: between a quarter and half past eleven – not as late as he had thought. All the same, he set off almost at a run, but had to settle down into a steady trot. His trotting footsteps on the road sounded clearly in the night quiet. But who was there to hear?

He neared the Challises' house. He drew level with it.

Ned Challis heard. Usually nothing woke him before the alarm-clock in the morning; but tonight footsteps woke him. Who, at this hour – he lifted the 23 back of his wrist towards his face, so that the time glimmered at him — who, at nearly twenty-five to twelve, could be hurrying along that road on foot? When the footsteps had almost gone — when it was already perhaps too late — he sprang out of bed and over to the window.

His wife woke. 'What's up, then, Ned?'

'Just somebody. I wondered who.'

'Oh, come back to bed!'

Ned Challis went back to bed; but almost at once got out again.

'Ned! What is it now?'

'I just thought I'd have a look at Lisa.'

At once Mrs Challis was wide awake. 'What's wrong with Lisa?'

'Nothing.' He went to listen at Lisa's door — listen to the regular, healthy breathing of her sleep. He came back. 'Nothing. Lisa's all right.'

'For heaven's sake! Why shouldn't she be?'

'Well, who was it walking out there? Hurrying.'

'Oh, go to sleep!'

24 'Yes.' He lay down again, drew the bedclothes

round him, lay still. But his eyes remained open.

Out in the night, Kevin left the road on which the Challises lived and came into the more important one that would take him into the village. He heard the rumble of a lorry coming up behind him. For safety he drew right into a gateway and waited. The lorry came past at a steady pace, headlights on. For a few seconds he saw the driver and his mate sitting up in the cab, intent on the road ahead. He had not wanted to be noticed by them, but, when they had gone, he felt lonely.

He went on into the village, its houses lightless, its streets deserted. By the entrance to the school driveway, he stopped to make sure he was unobserved. Nobody. Nothing — not even a cat. There was no sound of any vehicle now; but in the distance he heard a dog barking, and then another answered it. A little owl cried and cried for company or for sport. Then that, too, stopped.

He turned into the driveway to the school, and there was the gate to the playground. He looked over it, into the playground. Moonlight showed him everything: the expanse of asphalt, the sandpit, the big climbing-frame, and — at the far end — the fence with 25 the tussocks of grass growing blackly along it. It was all familiar, and yet strange because of the emptiness and the whitening of moonlight and the shadows cast like solid things. The climbing-frame reared high into the air, and on the ground stretched the black criss-cross of its shadows like the bars of a cage.

But he had not come all this way to be halted by moonshine and insubstantial shadows. In a businesslike way he climbed the gate and crossed the playground to the fence. He wondered whether he would find the right tussock easily, but he did. His fingers closed on the bottle: it was waiting for him.

At that moment, in the Challises' house, as they lay side by side in bed, Mrs Challis said to her husband: 'You're still awake, aren't you?'

'Yes.'

'What is it?'

'Nothing.'

Mrs Challis sighed.

'All right, then,' said Ned Challis. 'It's this. That bottle I gave Lisa – that little old bottle that I gave Lisa yesterday –'

'What about it?'

'I found it by Burnt House.'

Mrs Challis drew in her breath sharply. Then she said, 'That may mean nothing.' Then, 'How near was it?'

'Near enough.' After a pause: 'I ought never to have given it to Lisa. I never thought. But Lisa's all right, anyway.'

'But, Ned, don't you know what Lisa did with that bottle?'

'What?'

'Lent it to Kevin to have at school. And, according to her, he didn't return it when he should have done, on the way home. Didn't you hear her going on and on about it?'

'Kevin . . .' For the third time that night Ned Challis was getting out of bed, this time putting on his trousers, fumbling for his shoes. 'Somebody went up the road in a hurry. You know – I looked out. I couldn't see properly, but it was somebody small. It could have been a child. It could have been Lisa, but it wasn't. It could well have been Kevin . . .'

'Shouldn't you go to their house first, Ned – find 27

out whether Kevin is there or not? Make sure. You're not sure.'

'I'm not sure. But, if I wait to make sure, I may be too late.'

Mrs Challis did not say, 'Too late for what?' She did not argue.

Ned Challis dressed and went down. As he let himself out of the house to get his bicycle from the shed, the church clock began to strike the hour, the sound reaching him distantly across the intervening fields. He checked with his watch: midnight.

In the village, in the school playground, the striking of midnight sounded clangorously close. Kevin stood with the bottle held in the palm of his hand, waiting for the clock to stop striking – waiting as if for something to follow.

After the last stroke of midnight, there was silence, but Kevin still stood waiting and listening. A car or lorry passed the entrance of the school drive: he heard it distinctly; yet it was oddly faint, too. He couldn't place the oddness of it. It had sounded much further away than it should have done – less really there.

He gripped the bottle and went on listening, as if for some particular sound. The minutes passed. The same dog barked at the same dog, bark and reply — far, unreally far away. The little owl called; from another world, it might have been.

He was gripping the bottle so tightly now that his hand was sweating. He felt his skin begin to prickle with sweat at the back of his neck and under his arms.

Then there was a whistle from across the fields, distantly. It should have been an unexpected sound, just after midnight; but it did not startle him. It did set him off across the playground, however. Too late he wanted to get away. He had to go past the climbing-frame, whose cagework of shadows now stretched more largely than the frame itself. He saw the bars of shadow as he approached; he actually hesitated; and then, like a fool, he stepped inside the cage of shadows.

Ned Challis, on his bicycle, had reached the junction of the by-road with the road that — in one direction — led to the village. In the other it led 29 deeper into the country. Which way? He dismounted. He had to choose the right way – to follow Kevin.

Thinking of Whistlers' Hill, he turned the front wheel of his bicycle away from the village and set off again. But now, with his back to the village, going away from the village, he felt a kind of weariness and despair. A memory of childhood came into his mind: a game he had played in childhood: something hidden for him to find, and if he turned in the wrong direction to search, all the voices whispered to him, 'Cold – cold!' Now, with the village receding behind him, he recognized what he felt: cold . . . cold . . .

Without getting off his bicycle, he wheeled round and began to pedal hard in the direction of the village.

In the playground, there was no pressing hurry for Kevin any more. He did not press against the bars of his cage to get out. Even when clouds cut off the moonlight and the shadows melted into general darkness – even when the shadow-cage was no longer visible to the eye, he stood there; then crouched there, in a corner of the cage, as befitted a prisoner.

30

The church clock struck the quarter.

The whistlers were in no hurry. The first whistle had come from right across the fields. Then there was a long pause. Then the sound was repeated, equally distantly, from the direction of the river bridges. Later still, another whistle from the direction of the railway line, or somewhere near it.

He lay in his cage, cramped by the bars, listening. He did not know he was thinking, but suddenly it came to him: Whistlers' Hill. He and Lisa and the others had always supposed that the hill had belonged to a family called Whistler, as Challises' house belonged to the Challis family. But that was not how the hill had got its name – he saw that now. No, indeed not.

Whistler answered whistler at long intervals, like the sentries of a besieging army. There was no moving in as yet.

The church clock had struck the quarter as Ned Challis entered the village and cycled past the entrance to the school. He cycled as far as the Recreation Ground, perhaps because that was where Kevin would 31 have gone in the daytime. He cycled bumpily round the Ground: no Kevin.

He began to cycle back the way he had come, as though he had given up altogether and were going home. He cycled slowly. He passed the entrance to the school again.

In this direction, he was leaving the village. He was cycling so slowly that the front wheel of his bicycle wobbled desperately; the light from his dynamo was dim. He put a foot down and stopped. Motionless, he listened. There was nothing to hear, unless – yes, the faintest ghost of a sound, high pitched, prolonged for seconds, remote as from another world. Like a coward – and Ned Challis was no coward – he tried to persuade himself that he had imagined the sound; yet he knew he had not. It came from another direction now: very faint, yet penetrating, so that his skin crinkled to hear it. Again it came, from yet another quarter.

He wheeled his bicycle back to the entrance to the school and left it there. He knew he must be very close. He walked up to the playground gate and peered over it. But the moon was obscured by cloud: he could see nothing. He listened, waited for the moon to sail free.

In the playground Kevin had managed to get up, first on his hands and knees, then upright. He was very much afraid, but he had to be standing to meet whatever it was.

For the whistlers had begun to close in slowly, surely: converging on the school, on the school play-ground, on the cage of shadows. On him.

For some time now cloud-masses had obscured the moon. He could see nothing; but he felt the whistlers' presence. Their signals came more often, and always closer. Closer. Very close.

Suddenly the moon sailed free.

In the sudden moonlight Ned Challis saw clear across the playground to where Kevin stood against the climbing-frame, with his hands writhing together in front of him.

In the sudden moonlight Kevin did not see his uncle. Between him and the playground gate, and all round him, air was thickening into darkness. Frantic- 33 ally he tried to undo his fingers, that held the little bottle, so that he could throw it from him. But he could not. He held the bottle; the bottle held him.

The darkness was closing in on him. The darkness was about to take him; had surely got him.

Kevin shrieked.

Ned Challis shouted: 'I'm here!' and was over the gate and across the playground and with his arms round the boy: *'I've got you.'*

There was a tinkle as something fell from between Kevin's opened fingers: the little bottle fell and rolled to the middle of the playground. It lay there, very insignificant-looking.

Kevin was whimpering and shaking, but he could move of his own accord. Ned Challis helped him over the gate and to the bicycle.

'Do you think you could sit on the bar, Kev? Could you manage that?'

'Yes.' He could barely speak.

Ned Challis hesitated, thinking of the bottle which had chosen to come to rest in the very centre of the playground, where the first child tomorrow would see it, pick it up.

He went back and picked the bottle up. Wherever he threw it, someone might find it. He might smash it and grind the pieces underfoot; but he was not sure he dared to do that.

Anyway, he was not going to hold it in his hand longer than he strictly must. He put it into his pocket, and then, when he got back to Kevin and the bicycle, he slipped it into the saddle-bag.

He rode Kevin home on the cross-bar of his bicycle. At the Challises' front gate Mrs Challis was waiting, with the dog for company. She just said: 'He all right then?'

'Ah.'

'I'll make a cup of tea while you take him home.'

At his own front door, Kevin said: 'I left the door on the latch. I can get in. I'm all right. I'd rather – I'd rather – '

'Less spoken of, the better,' said his uncle. 'You go to bed. Nothing to be afraid of now.'

He waited until Kevin was inside the house and

he heard the latch click into place. Then he rode back to his wife, his cup of tea, and consideration of the problem that lay in his saddle-bag.

After he had told his wife everything, and they had discussed possibilities, Ned Challis said thoughtfully: 'I might take it to the museum, after all. Safest place for it would be inside a glass case there.'

'But you said they wouldn't want it.'

'Perhaps they would, if I told them where I found it and a bit – only a bit – about Burnt House . . .'

'You do that, then.'

Ned Challis stood up and yawned with a finality that said, Bed.

'But don't you go thinking you've solved all your problems by taking that bottle to Castleford, Ned. Not by a long chalk.'

'No?'

'Lisa. She reckons she owns that bottle.'

'I'll deal with Lisa tomorrow.'

'Today, by the clock.'

36   Ned Challis gave a groan that turned into another

yawn. 'Bed first,' he said; 'then Lisa.' They went to bed not long before the dawn.

The next day and for days after that, Lisa was furiously angry with her father. He had as good as stolen her bottle, she said, and now he refused to give it back, to let her see it, even to tell her what he had done with it. She was less angry with Kevin. (She did not know, of course, the circumstances of the bottle's passing from Kevin to her father.)

Kevin kept out of Lisa's way, and even more carefully kept out of his uncle's. He wanted no private conversation.

One Saturday Kevin was having tea at the Challises', because he had been particularly invited. He sat with Lisa and Mrs Challis. Ned had gone to Castleford, and came in late. He joined them at the tea-table in evident good spirits. From his pocket he brought out a small cardboard box, which he placed in the centre of the table, by the Saturday cake. His wife was staring at him: before he spoke, he gave her the slightest nod of reassurance. 'The museum didn't want to keep that little old glass bottle, after all,' he said. 37

Both the children gave a cry: Kevin started up with such a violent backward movement that his chair clattered to the floor behind him; Lisa leant forward, her fingers clawing towards the box.

'No!' Ned Challis said. To Lisa he added: 'There it stays, girl, till *I* say.' To Kevin: 'Calm down. Sit up at the table again and listen to me.' Kevin picked his chair up and sat down again, resting his elbows on the table, so that his hands supported his head.

'Now,' said Ned Challis, 'you two know so much that it's probably better you should know more. That little old bottle came from Whistlers' Hill, below Burnt House – well, you know that. Burnt House is only a ruin now – elder bushes growing inside as well as out; but once it was a cottage that someone lived in. Your mother's granny remembered the last one to live there.'

'No, Ned,' said Mrs Challis, 'it was my great-granny remembered.'

'Anyway,' said Ned Challis, 'it was so long ago that Victoria was the Queen, that's certain. And an old woman lived alone in that cottage. There were stories about her.'

'Was she a witch?' breathed Lisa.

'So they said. They said she went out on the hillside at night —'

'At the full of the moon,' said Mrs Challis.

'They said she dug up roots and searched out plants and toadstools and things. They said she caught rats and toads and even bats. They said she made ointments and powders and weird brews. And they said she used what she made to cast spells and call up spirits.'

'Spirits from Hell, my great-granny said. Real bad 'uns.'

'So people said, in the village. Only the parson scoffed at the whole idea. Said he'd called often and been shown over the cottage and seen nothing out of the ordinary — none of the jars and bottles of stuff that she was supposed to have for her witchcraft. He said she was just a poor cranky old woman; that was all.

'Well, she grew older and older and crankier and crankier, and one day she died. Her body lay in its coffin in the cottage, and the parson was going to bury her next day in the churchyard.

'The night before she was to have been buried, someone went up from the village –'

'Someone!' said Mrs Challis scornfully. 'Tell them the whole truth, Ned, if you're telling the story at all. Half the village went up, with lanterns – men, women, and children. Go on, Ned.'

'The cottage was thatched, and they began to pull swatches of straw away and take it into the cottage and strew it round and heap it up under the coffin. They were going to fire it all.

'They were pulling the straw on the downhill side of the cottage when suddenly a great piece of thatch came away and out came tumbling a whole lot of things that the old woman must have kept hidden there. People did hide things in thatches, in those days.'

'Her savings?' asked Lisa.

'No. A lot of jars and little bottles, all stoppered or sealed, neat and nice. With stuff inside.'

There was a silence at the tea-table. Then Lisa said: 'That proved it: she was a witch.'

40 'Well, no, it only proved she *thought* she was a

witch. That was what the parson said afterwards – and whew! was he mad when he knew about that night.'

Mrs Challis said: 'He gave it 'em red hot from the pulpit the next Sunday. He said that once upon a time poor old deluded creatures like her had been burnt alive for no reason at all, and the village ought to be ashamed of having burnt her dead.'

Lisa went back to the story of the night itself. 'What did they do with what came out of the thatch?'

'Bundled it inside the cottage among the straw, and fired it all. The cottage burnt like a beacon that night, they say. Before cockcrow, everything had been burnt to ashes. That's the end of the story.'

'Except for my little bottle,' said Lisa. 'That came out of the thatch, but it didn't get picked up. It rolled downhill, or someone kicked it.'

'That's about it,' Ned agreed.

Lisa stretched her hand again to the cardboard box, and this time he did not prevent her. But he said: 'Don't be surprised, Lisa. It's different.'

She paused. 'A different bottle?'

'The same bottle, but – well, you'll see.'

Lisa opened the box, lifted the packaging of cotton wool, took the bottle out. It was the same bottle, but the stopper had gone, and it was empty and clean – so clean that it shone greenly. Innocence shone from it.

'You said the stopper would never come out,' Lisa said slowly.

'They forced it by suction. The museum chap wanted to know what was inside, so he got the hospital lab to take a look – he has a friend there. It was easy for them.'

Mrs Challis said: 'That would make a pretty vase, Lisa. For tiny flowers.' She coaxed Lisa to go out to pick a posy from the garden; she herself took the bottle away to fill it with water.

Ned Challis and Kevin faced each other across the table.

Kevin said: 'What was in it?'

Ned Challis said: 'A trace of this, a trace of that, the hospital said. One thing more than anything else.'

'Yes?'

'Blood. Human blood.'

Lisa came back with her flowers; Mrs Challis came back with the bottle filled with water. When the flowers had been put in, it looked a pretty thing.

'My witch-bottle,' said Lisa contentedly. 'What was she called – the old woman that thought she was a witch?'

Her father shook his head; her mother thought: 'Madge – or was it Maggy –?'

'Maggy Whistler's bottle, then,' said Lisa.

'Oh, no,' said Mrs Challis. 'She was Maggy – or Madge – Dawson. I remember my granny saying so. Dawson.'

'Then why's it called Whistlers' Hill?'

'I'm not sure,' said Mrs Challis uneasily. 'I mean, I don't think anyone knows for certain.'

But Ned Challis, looking at Kevin's face, knew that he knew for certain.

Her Father's Attic

ROSAMUND was an only child, and the apple of her mother's eye. She resembled her mother: pink cheeked, golden haired, blue eyed. She was going to be like her mother: pretty.

Mrs Brunning had faith in her daughter's looks. 'She'll be picked out,' she said. 'She'll go up to London and be a model. Or go on telly. She'll make a name for herself, and money; and marry well . . . What did you say, Geoff?'

But Mr Brunning, who was hungry from working out of doors, had only grunted: his attention was entirely on his dinner. Besides, he knew the kind of thing that would come next.

'Anyway,' his wife said, 'she won't hang about here until some drudging clodhopper marries her, and she has to end her days where she began 'em.'

This was a dig at her husband, who was a small farmer and an unsuccessful one: he worked hard on his land for very little return. He had inherited his father's farm and farmhouse only because none of his four elder brothers had wanted to: they had had higher ambitions, and achieved them. He had been the runt of the family, small, sallow, timid; he had been teased and persecuted all his childhood. He had married – so his wife considered – above him; and he would be teased and persecuted for the rest of his married life.

'Rosamund has more of me in her than she has of you, thank goodness,' said Mrs Brunning. 'She's all me, is Rosamund.'

Rosamund, above whose head her mother wrangled, yawned inside her mouth and was glad that dinner was over. Her father got up and went back to his work outside, and Mrs Brunning began washing up. There was no question of Rosamund's helping: she was the only child, spoilt, her mother's darling. Mrs Brunning considered most of the local children unfit company for her; so, as often before, Rosamund went off now to play alone indoors. Indoors, because her mother hated farm-filth, as she called it, ever to be on her feet.

Brunning's was an old house, although without any particular history – Geoffrey Brunning could say only that his father knew that *his* father had been born there. It was not at all a grand house, but it had been built for a time of many children and of farm-servants living with their masters. Nowadays there were shut rooms and unused passageways, away from the central, lived-in part of the house; such outlying parts suffered the erosions of neglect and time. Since Geoffrey Brunning's childhood, for instance, the highest attic, once a nursery, had been closed. Mr Brunning said the floor was unsafe, and – particularly to safeguard Rosamund – had locked the door that opened to the attic stairway.

So the door was already locked before Rosamund was old enough to roam the house on her own, and soon after that the woodworm had begun their invisible banquet upon the framework. Rosamund used regularly to bang at the closed door as she passed it, but without real curiosity. Perhaps her knock interrupted the woodworms' gnawing for a moment; then they resumed. Neither she nor they, after the

passage of years, were at all prepared for the day –
this very day – when their world exploded in a flurry
of wood-dust, as her casual blow sent the metalwork
of the lock right through the decayed woodwork of
the frame. Abruptly the door swung open as if to
open wide, then its hinges creaked to a rusty standstill,
and Rosamund was left with a sliced-off view of
wooden stairs powdered with old plaster and new
wood-dust.

Of course, Rosamund had always known of the
existence of the attic, but the opening of the way to it
was new. She must – she *must* go up and see it for
herself. Circumstances were favourable: her father
was out on the farm; her mother would still be in the
kitchen, either finishing washing up or beginning to
prepare for a genteel visitor that afternoon. Between
the kitchen and the attic lay a wasteland of empty
rooms and passages. Rosamund listened carefully, but
she could hear no sound from anywhere.

She took a deeper breath than usual, and pushed
firmly against the door. It offered surprising resistance,
but finally opened wide enough to allow her body to 47

pass through. She began going carefully up into the darkness of the stairway, feeling before her with her hands.

At the top of the stairs, she stubbed her fingers against another door. It had a small round hole at the level of a handle, but a spider had been at work and her peeping eye could see only a mesh illumined from beyond by a dim lemon-coloured light.

For the first time, with darkness round her, and the unbroken silence of years, she nearly felt afraid, but would not allow the feeling to grow upon her. She pressed very softly at the door. At once, with a kind of over-eagerness, the door swung right back.

She stood on the threshold of her father's attic-nursery. Its bare length stretched uninterruptedly from her feet to a small window at the far end, where the afternoon sunlight shone weakly through dusty glass, greenish yellow where the last leaves of a creeper encroached upon the panes.

She was not afraid now. Being a practical child, she first considered the floor, which her father had

said was unsafe. The bare boards looked firm, and she

began to test them, one after another. They bore her weight. She knew that she was not as heavy as a grown-up person, yet she felt beneath her feet the solid assurance of timber that would outlast generations. The floor was sound, when her father had said it was not: she felt puzzled.

There was no other mystery to the room. It was quite empty, except for the low shelves and cupboards that had been built into the steep angle where the sloping roof met the floor. She examined the cupboards carefully: they were all quite empty, even the one with the door that appeared to be locked but was only jammed. Someone, at some time, had forced the door, and damaged it. Delicately she eased it open. She left that door standing ajar, because it had been so difficult. She might want to get in again. The cupboard was a roomy one, without shelves.

Rosamund went to the window next. With the stubbornness of disuse, it refused to open; but she cleared a pane of glass and could look through. She was charmed with the novelty of the view from here. She looked right across the roofs of the farm-buildings 49 to the fields and the spire of the parish church beyond. She thought that she could distinguish her father at work in one of the middle fields, but the light was failing. The setting sun stood in irregular red slices behind a thin copse of trees on the skyline.

Having gazed for so long into the last of the sun, she was surprised at the darkness of the room when she turned back to it. Shadows had gathered thickly at the far end, by the door; and inky blackness had settled in the depth of the one cupboard left open. She decided suddenly that it was time to leave the attic.

She started off across the safe, safe floor towards the stairway that led back to the peopled part of the house.

The attic was a long one and Rosamund walked slowly, because still with that careful, light step – she could not quite put from her mind the idea that the place was dangerous. She drew level with the open cupboard, and looked deeply into it. She halted as it occurred to her – without surprise or pleasure – that this cupboard would make a good hiding-place: it was large enough for a child of her age, crouching.

Neither excitement nor pleasure; neither surprise nor speculation – she seemed to have remembered the possibilities of the cupboard, rather than freshly to have thought of them.

There she stood, staring into the cupboard.

The sun had gone, and the shadows of the room moved up towards the window. They lapped round Rosamund like a sea and she began to sink into them like a drowning person.

She sank to the floor and lay along it, quite still. Her eyes were wide open, fixed upon the darkness in the cupboard. Darkness and fear flowed from the cupboard and filled the attic from doorway to window.

Outside in the field Geoffrey Brunning was still working in the afterlight. Now he stopped abruptly: he told himself he had forgotten that he must go in early today. He must go.

He had forgotten nothing; but it was as if something had remembered *him*. He did not know why he was going – why he was hurrying. As he neared the farmhouse he broke into an awkward, anxious trot.

He went in by the back door as usual, leaving his boots there, and so into the kitchen. It was empty and almost dark except for the red glow from the old-fashioned stove that his wife was always complaining about.

'Ros!' he called. There was no answer.

He decided to have some commonsense. He switched on the light, filled the kettle and put it on to boil, and began to cut bread for toast. He cut one slice, then laid the knife carefully down and went to stand out in the hall. It was dark there, with only a line of light from underneath the door of the sitting-room. That was where his wife would be entertaining. He could hear voices, but not Rosamund's. He had not expected to hear it.

He turned away from the door of the sitting-room, as he had turned away from the kitchen; and now he faced the main stairs. In the dark he could hardly see them. He stood peering, trying to make his mind work commonsensically; to think of the electric light switch that would banish darkness. But darkness increased moment by moment, filling his mind. Darkness and fear flowed round him like a sea, rose round him to drown him.

He gave a cry and turned quickly back to the light of the kitchen. Then, at the very door, he swerved aside and set off at a rush, but not firmly; stumbling and feeling like a blind man up the stairs, along walls, round corners. His course was directly up and towards the disused attic.

At the threshold of the attic he took a deep breath, like a man about to enter a smoke-filled room. He could see nothing, but he knew that Rosamund was there. He made one mistake, in thinking – in being sure – that she would be crouching in the cupboard with the jammed door. Even as his feet felt their way towards it, they met her body on the floor. He bent, took hold of her, and dragged her to the top of the attic stairway; then, having gathered her in his arms, he carried her down and away, to the kitchen. There he set her upon a chair, where she began to stir and blink in the bright light, like a dreamer waking; but she had not been asleep. She was very pale at first, but soon the pink began to reappear in her cheeks. 53

She did not speak to her father, but her awakened gaze never left him.

Her father had collapsed upon another chair in the kitchen.

There Mrs Brunning found them, having said good-bye to her visitor. Her daughter seemed as usual, but her husband was leaning forward in an attitude of exhaustion, his fingers dangling over the edge of his knees, his face white and sweaty.

'Don't say you're sickening for something, now!' Mrs Brunning said sharply. 'You're a sight! What do you feel like?'

'Oh . . . I feel . . .'

What did he feel like?

Long ago, when he was a child, he had felt like this, once. His brothers had shut him into one of the nursery cupboards, just for their fun; and the cupboard door had jammed. That was all it had been, except for the darkness inside the cupboard; and his fear. The darkness and the fear had lasted for ever. They said afterwards that his being shut in had all lasted only a short time, and that he had been stupid to be so afraid. They'd been able to force the cupboard door open in the end, and then they'd dragged him out. But the darkness had stayed behind in the cupboard; and his fear.

'Well, what do you feel like?' his wife repeated irritably.

'Nothing special.'

'Let's hope you pass nothing special on to Rosamund, then. But at least she's not one of those easy-ailing children. Like me, in that.'

Rosamund was staring at her father, paying no attention to her mother's refrain: 'Yes, more of me in her than you, thank goodness. All me.' Rosamund was staring at her father as at somebody strange to her, and of the strangest importance.

Penguin Children's 60s

ALI BABA AND THE FORTY THIEVES • *Retold by N. J. Dawood*
THE AMAZING PIPPI LONGSTOCKING • *Astrid Lindgren*
ANNE AT GREEN GABLES • *L. M. Montgomery*
AT THE RIVER-GATES AND
OTHER SUPERNATURAL STORIES • *Philippa Pearce*
CLASSIC GHOST STORIES
CLASSIC NONSENSE VERSE
THE CLOCKWORK MOUSE • *Dick King-Smith*
DEAD MAN'S LANE • *Joan Aiken*
THE DRAGON ON THE ROOF • *Terry Jones*
FOUR GREAT GREEK MYTHS • *Roger Lancelyn Green*
THE GREAT MOUSE PLOT AND
OTHER TALES OF CHILDHOOD • *Roald Dahl*
THE GREAT TIME WARP ADVENTURE • *Jon Scieszka*
THE HOOLIGAN'S SHAMPOO • *Philip Ridley*
KEEP IT IN THE FAMILY • *Anne Fine*
KING ARTHUR'S COURT • *Roger Lancelyn Green*
THE LITTLE MERMAID AND
OTHER FAIRY TALES • *Hans Andersen (Translated by Naomi Lewis)*
LOST DOG AND OTHER STORIES • *Penelope Lively*
THE MIDNIGHT STORY • *Margaret Mahy*
MOOMINTROLLS AND FRIENDS • *Tove Jansson*
MRS PEPPERPOT TURNS DETECTIVE • *Alf Prøysen*
THE NIGHT TRAIN: STORIES IN PROSE AND VERSE • *Allan Ahlberg*
THE PIED PIPER OF HAMELIN AND OTHER CLASSIC STORIES IN VERSE
ROBIN HOOD AND HIS MERRY MEN • *Roger Lancelyn Green*
SHERLOCK HOLMES AND THE SPECKLED BAND • *Sir Arthur Conan Doyle*
SMACKING MY LIPS • *Michael Rosen*
TALES FROM ALICE IN WONDERLAND • *Lewis Carroll*
TALES FROM THE JUNGLE BOOK • *Rudyard Kipling*
THREE QUIRKY TAILS • *Paul Jennings*
TOM SAWYER'S PIRATE ADVENTURE • *Mark Twain*
TOM THUMB AND OTHER FAIRY TALES • *Jacob and Wilhelm Grimm*